ECHOES OF THE ASCENDED
BY GELINEAU AND KING

A Reaper of Stone
Rend the Dark
Best Left in the Shadows
Faith and Moonlight
Broken Banners (coming soon)

PRAISE FOR BEST LEFT IN THE SHADOWS

"I was blown away by the detail and world building that was accomplished in so few pages. I didn't feel like I was seeing a section of a puzzle, more like I was reading a story that would contribute to a larger whole, but is compelling and rich all on its own."

– Mama Reads, Hazel Sleeps

"Like with the previous *Ascended* books, I really love the characters and their dynamic. The female lead Alys is different from the heroines in *Reaper* and *Rend the Dark*, but she's just as complex and strong."

– White Sky Project

"The story was filled with gritty characters and dirty back streets, lies and deception. There was also this great sexual tension between Alys and Daxton that created a witty banter, which was so much fun to read."

– Paein and Ms4Tune

Praise for Faith and Moonlight

"*Faith and Moonlight* is reminiscent of Terry Pratchett in that laced through the heavy atmosphere, array of emotion, and implausible magic is hope. That spirit of what might be lightens the feel considerablely, making for a delightful story."

– Rabid Readers Reviews

"Amazing, well-developed, and relatable characters combines with snappy, realistic dialogue and simple prose to make this coming of age story... a true fantasy gem."

– Cover2Cover

"A heartbreaking narrative that was so realistic at times, I forgot I was reading fantasy."

– Mama Reads, Hazel Sleeps

"You can really feel Roan's desire and dream to be something more and you can also feel Kay's frustration and struggle. And underneath all that you can practically touch how much they care about each other."

– White Sky Project

MARK GELINEAU
JOE KING

BEST LEFT
IN THE
SHADOWS

AN ECHO OF THE ASCENDED

First Printing: November 2015

v1.0

Gelineau and King

ISBN 978-1-944015-05-3

www.gelineauandking.com

ACKNOWLEDGMENTS

Mark: A huge thank you to my dad, Dan Gelineau, my brother Dave, my wife Tiffany, and my son Bryce for their love and devotion. And to my mom, Pam Gelineau, who I miss every day.

Joe: To Irene, Emma, and Kate. Thank you. You guys make me a better everything.

A massive thanks to the team that helped put it all together: Jason, TJ, and Marija.

And also to our friends and beta readers: Jason, Maria, Dave, Helen, Maggie, and Emily.

ACT 1
A MESSY LITTLE MURDER

The slow lapping of the Prion River mingled with the creaking wood symphony of the water wheel beside the dock. Moonlight tinted the heavy fog as the last hours of night became the first hours of morning. The heavy mist lay upon the woman's corpse, fat drops of dew sitting on the blood and making it shine.

Alys bent over the body, her hands on her hips as she studied the dead woman's face. Young. Roughed up. She may have been pretty once, but it was impossible to tell now. Old bruises and new mixed with dried blood to create a mask over the girl's features.

Alys turned to the man standing against the wooden wall of the pier and shrugged. "What do you want me to say?"

The man finished speaking to a pair of city guards and waited until the two men clanked away in their armored breastplates and shiny helms. His light hair, always cropped close and crisply perfect, shone briefly in the glow from the torches the guards carried. Alys caught just a glimpse of those familiar blue eyes before the light from the torches faded away.

He pulled his long coat closer about him against the chill of the morning. The black fabric and gray striping of a royal magistrate made him stand out.

She corrected her thoughts. *Stand out even more.*

"I want you to tell me what happened," he said.

She laughed, adjusting the large-bladed scythe that she carried across her back. "What happened? Someone killed her, Magistrate Inspector Daxton Ellis," Alys said, punctuating every syllable of the man's title with a clipped enunciation.

He gave her a long, hard stare. "Nothing is ever easy with you, is it, Alys?"

"It's part of my charm," she said, moving over to the wall beside him. As she drew closer, she studied his face – the subtle play of muscles around his eyes, the set of his mouth. He was always easy to read. "You know who she is." It was not a question.

He hesitated at first, then said, "She's Lydia Ashdown."

"Old name," she said.

"Old everything."

Alys shrugged. "Doesn't mean much down here in Lowside. You're sure it's her?"

The inspector gave her a slow nod. "She's been missing for three months now. The parents held out hope that she had just had a rebellious jaunt out to the marches to visit friends or relatives." He shook his head. "Still, the magistrates were given her description. We knew there was a chance we'd find her like this, but there was always hope. At least until tonight."

Alys flicked her tongue against her teeth in silent annoyance. "That doesn't answer my question, Dax. How do you know this is her?"

"When she was younger, she was playing and fell into the hearth," he said. "It left her with a burn scar between her..." He cleared his throat. "Over her heart area."

2

Alys laughed. "So you tore open this poor girl's bodice for your salacious gaze? Why Dax, you cad!"

"The mark is distinctive. It looks like a sparrow."

"A sparrow?" Alys said in disbelief, kneeling down and opening up the corpse's shirt. Underneath the clothing, on the stiff, waxy flesh was a brownish red mark. It sat between her breasts, just over her heart. To Alys's surprise, it actually did look quite a bit like a sparrow in flight. "Amazing. Highside even has prettier scars than we do."

"This is hardly a laughing matter, Alys. The Ashdowns are true blooded. They have a direct line to the First Ascended. And their daughter is dead. In Lowside."

"Ah," Alys said. "And there it is. I was wondering what had prompted the chief magistrate to assign you here, dear Dax. Now, I know. You true bloods stick together, right? They brought you in to tidy things up and make sure the Ashdown family is confident that a person of the correct breeding and background is investigating the death of their poor child."

His eyes narrowed. "I thought we weren't making this personal?" he remarked, an edge in his voice. "Wasn't that one of the rules?" He paused and shook his head. "I'm not here to tidy anything up. I am here for justice. To find who is responsible. It does not matter to me in the slightest how true hers or anyone's blood may be. You should know that most of all." He looked at her and in his eyes was that familiar look of resolution, but also a bit of challenge as well.

That was new.

Silently, she cursed him. As ever, he knew all the right buttons to push. And he was right. Those were the rules. Keep it business. Alys presented a charming smile to him. "A noble endeavor, Dax. And one I would be glad to assist you with, but you know that nothing is free, Magistrate Inspector. Especially down here in Lowside."

"The city will pay for your assistance. Discretely, of course."

"I don't need coin. I can steal whatever coin I want." He remained quiet at that, and she chuckled. "Oh come now, Daxton. Surely it hasn't been so long you can't remember what a girl really wants?"

"I can't do it. You know I can't." But even as he spoke, Alys saw his eyes move back to the body before them.

The way his attention kept returning to the corpse, the way his breath came a little faster as she was about to move away. This was a serious case. A Highside victim, old family nobility, found in Prionside. Dax was out of his element here and he knew it.

"What do you want to know?" he said at last.

Alys moved in closer and whispered in his ear. "The appointment for Justicar of the Second District is coming. I want to know who's going to get the nod for that post and what leverage the appointers have on them."

Dax spun away. "You're out of your damned mind."

"Oh, unclench. You know I will be discreet, Dax. I always am."

"It hasn't been fully decided yet," Dax said through tight lips.

Alys waggled a finger in front of him. "Stop trying to avoid it. This is no small endeavor you are asking me to join you on. And knowing who's getting tapped should just about cover it. The Second District Justicar is the law in Lowside." She paused and smiled at him. "Well, the king's law, anyway."

He did not smile back. If anything, his frown seemed to intensify. "It's not you that I don't trust, Alys. It's who you'll sell the information to."

"Believe me, Dax. They know the rules too," she said. "This is their world. One that they carved out for themselves and built with sweat and blood. They're not going to shit on all that."

Alys met his gaze with her own dark eyes. She saw him break first, unable to keep from looking at the corpse. Inside, she smiled.

"Fine. I will find out what you want, but I will want results first."

"Of course," she said.

She pressed her hand against her heart and then held it out to him. He did the same and they clasped forearms, sealing the deal.

"The Ashdowns will want someone to answer for this," Dax said. "They will look to the top and think that Blacktide Harry himself is involved," he said.

"No chance it's Harry," she said.

"He's still boss in Prionside District, right? The Stevedore Rats still answer to him?"

"Why Magistrate Inspector! It seems you have been keeping an ear to the ground in regards to the goings on of the shade folk."

"It's his domain," he said. "And he's got the reputation for violence."

"Oh Harry's as black-hearted a bastard as you'll ever meet, but he has no temper. Everything he does is cold. But even more, this," she said, pointing to the body of the young woman, "is bad for business. It's public. It shines a light on Prionside. The Blacktide would never do anything to disrupt business on the docks. Never."

"Well, then if he is so innocent, he shouldn't mind the inconvenience of a few questions, should he?" He fixed her with a look that slowly evolved into a smile. "You can arrange a meeting, can't you?"

"You're wasting time," Alys said, reaching back and adjusting the large scythe in its harness, and checking the daggers at her belt. "But I suppose, if you are set on it, it wouldn't hurt to pay him a visit anyway. If you really want to follow this, we'll need the Blacktide's blessing if we're going to be poking around Prionside."

With that, she offered him her arm. "Come along, Magistrate Inspector. It's late at night, and the streets can be so very dangerous," she said, batting her eyes at him. "An escort is ever so important."

Dax frowned again, but behind his eyes, Alys caught just the barest hint of amusement. "Then I suppose it is good that I have one," he said.

ACT 2
IN THE COURT OF THE BLACKTIDE

"Watch your head," Alys warned.

Dax was so focused on poling the small, flat-bottomed skiff along the canal that he had not noticed the low arch at the tunnel entrance. He muttered a curse as he ducked down, avoiding smacking his head on the mold-covered brick. The top of the pole scraped along the ceiling as they entered the dark tunnel.

"You're enjoying this aren't you, Alys?"

Alys smiled, reclining on the floor of the skiff, and shrugged. "What more could a girl ask for than a lovely moonlight canal ride?" she asked. "Of course, now that we've entered the Sumpworks, we can't see the moon. And the water smells like rotting fish and a week's worth of shit. But still..." She closed her eyes and waved a hand lazily in the air. "Lovely."

"You're the one who took us this route, remember?"

"That's because I remember your fondness for slumming it," Alys replied. There was a slight edge to her voice, and Dax recognized the shot for what it was.

There was a time he would have snapped back, railing against her insinuation. But not tonight. He was here to do a job, and he needed Alys for it, and the memories of the past, sweet and suffering alike, would only complicate things. And Lydia Ashdown deserved more than that. The girl was dead and he would be damned sure to find out who had done it and why.

And yet, he could not stop looking at Alys. She seemed more beautiful, more alive than he could ever remember. She had changed her hair. It was longer now, beads and ribbons woven into braids that writhed like serpents when she moved. But those eyes, dark and full of secrets, were still the same as they had always been, and they pulled him to her, just as they always had. Since the moment she had walked onto the docks, he wanted to reach out and hold her the way he once had.

But he didn't.

He couldn't.

Instead, he held his tongue and pushed them through the shit and water and focused on the present.

She seemed to pick up on his quiet. "You sure you want to do this?"

"I've met the Blacktide before."

She craned her neck back to look at him. "That was a long time ago. Harry isn't small time anymore. He's the boss of all of Prionside now. One of Pious Black's Thirteen."

At the name, Dax felt the blood drain from his face. "You still answer to Pious Black?" he asked, his voice tight.

"You still answer to your father?" she shot back immediately.

And just like that, he felt sixteen again. Young, naive, unbearably in love, and twice as ashamed. Dax tried to will himself to keep staring at her, but ultimately, he turned his head away.

For a moment, there was only the sound of lapping water. Then, he heard Alys sigh deeply. "Shit, Dax. Let's not do this again."

He gripped the pole tighter. "Believe me. I wouldn't be here if I had any other choice," he said.

She gave a small laugh. "Nice," she replied.

"Do you want the truth, Alys? Or would you prefer we keep it all delicate and civil?" He could not keep the bitter edge from his voice.

She gave him a look, one eyebrow raised. "You've changed. I like it, but if you are insisting on honesty, then yes, let's be honest." She gestured with a finger, pointing back and forth between the two of them. "This isn't going to end well."

Dax frowned. "Why not? We've been able to put aside the past before. You helped me catch that piece of filth that was burning those merchant ships."

"That wasn't what I meant. And anyway, that was a damn sight different than this. That was a small-time gutter runner who liked to watch the flames dance. This," she said, gesturing ahead of them down the darkened tunnel, "this is a Lowside boss, and you're talking about stomping around in his domain."

"All the more reason he should cooperate then. If the ports get shut down and Prionside closed off, it will look bad for him."

"Those are big, bold words, Magistrate Inspector. And an awfully serious road to walk for a random Highside girl. I don't care how old or true her name might be." She scrutinized him for a long moment, her eyes shining in the low light from the flickering torches lining the walls. "You knew her," she said.

He kept his eyes on the water and the dark shadows of the tunnel. "I met her a few times when she was very little. I know her sister, Kara. She was at the collegium the same time you and

I were. A year below us. I don't think you would remember her, though."

Alys settled back down into the bottom of the skiff. "I try my very hardest to not remember those times," she said with a smile.

"Me too," he said honestly, "but Kara reached out to me three months ago, when Lydia first disappeared. She said her sister had been seeing someone the family did not approve of. Lower status."

From her reclined position, Alys raised a hand twirled it around. "Sounds like the intricacies of Highside romance."

"That's what I thought. I looked everywhere Highside. Talked to everyone." As he spoke, Dax felt his grip tighten on the wooden pole until his fingers ached. "I was certain she'd turn up somewhere in Highside." The image of the body on the docks flashed through his mind. "I was wrong."

He was glad she was facing away from him. She could read him too well, and he did not want her to see that those last words were a lie.

Thoughts of Lydia in Lowside had not started this morning with the body. He had felt it early on. Had known deep down that whoever Lydia had fallen for wasn't from Highside, but there had been no one he could contact in Lowside. No one he could turn to.

No one except Alys.

And he hadn't been able to do it. Hadn't been able to open that door again and face that kind of pain once more. Not on a hunch.

And because of his cowardice, Lydia Ashdown was dead. Murdered on a Lowside dock.

"Well," Alys replied, her voice cutting through his thoughts. "That's why we're going to the Blacktide. If you want me to start digging into every dark and seedy little corner of the district, I need his permission to do it." There was a brief pause before she spoke, and then a slight edge of warning to her words. "Just try to keep that righteous passion for justice on a leash. Your pretty gray stripes mean nothing down here. The king's protection means nothing. Down here, Blacktide Harry is king."

"I'm not here to play games, Alys. I'm here to get this done. Right and quickly." He had to duck his tall head to avoid striking it on yet another low hanging archway and the skiff rocked. "This is the only way in?" he said, blowing out a frustrated breath.

"There are other ways in to the Sumpworks, but this way is the front door," she said. "Where guests come knocking. And if you haven't been summoned, you come announced as a guest. That's a rule."

Dax kept moving the skiff forward with the pole. "Announced?"

"Yes, announced. We were marked back on the docks, and as soon as we started down the canal, they've been watching us." Ahead of them, the darkness of the tunnel ended in greasy yellow light. "Alright, Dax, besides the sword at your side, the short blade at your belt, and that dagger in your boot you think no one notices, what other weapons do you have on you?"

Dax glanced down toward his right boot with a grimace. "That's all I'm carrying."

Alys clucked her tongue. "Much too light a load for night work down Lowside, but maybe that's for the best right now," she said. "Keep your hands on the pole and keep the pole in the water. Make no moves toward any of your weapons. No matter what."

Gesturing with his chin toward the large scythe strapped to her back, he smirked. "Do you think that they will even be looking at me with that horror you got back there?"

"Me and Aunty," she said, reaching back to pat the scythe, "are known quantities here. You, on the other hand, are a Royal Magistrate coming armed to a boss's den. Do not forget that."

As they drew toward the light, Dax tried to keep his eyes opened wide to force them to adjust more quickly. They drifted past the final arch and into a huge space featuring wooden scaffolds in varying stages of rot, laid over the brickwork of the walls.

The canal continued straight through the large room, but small walkways spanned the canal. On each, rough-looking men and women watched them. All had a crossbow close at hand.

"The fact that they aren't leveled at us already is a very auspicious sign for this meeting," Alys whispered from the corner of her mouth, her lips not fully moving.

At the far end of the space, the brick foundations jutted out over the canal, and the water passed through a colossal grate. Upon that brick platform, seated upon a towering throne constructed from wooden crates and netting, was the Blacktide himself.

His dark hair was slicked back and looked wet, like living amid the water of the Prion had changed him. Gotten into his blood. It gleamed an oily black, as did the thick mustache he affected. His eyes were cold blue amidst the weathered and wrinkled face, and they watched the skiff approach without blinking.

"Hello, Uncle Harry," Alys said, with her brightest smile. She extended her hands to her sides and curtsied delicately.

"You were never short of sand, girl. I figured you would be drifting in, with everything else washing up on my shores tonight." His eyes shifted past her to Dax, then his attention focused back to Alys. "Didn't know you two were sharing company again."

"Just business, Uncle Harry," she said. "He's come down to Prionside for a case. Fortunately, he was not required to bring any friends with him. For now," she said. "A single tourist is one thing, but a crowd of them, well, that would be another thing entirely."

The Blacktide settled back onto the wooden throne, pouring himself a drink. "Your thoughts and mine, as was often the case, do seem to move along a similar course," he said before knocking back the drink.

"It's a bad situation Uncle Harry," she said. "High profile trouble on the docks, and any answers you find will be deemed a bit too convenient, would they not?"

"They would indeed. They would indeed," the Blacktide said. "Which is why I figured you'd be coming. You always smelled opportunity like it was blood in the water."

"I learned from the best."

In response, the Blacktide raised his glass in salute and drank once more. "A girl left on my docks, just a few feet from the water that would have erased all trace of the body." He settled back in his throne. "No simple murder."

"She was a message then."

"I assume as much. But it wasn't meant for me."

At that, Dax spoke up, "For whom, then?"

Blacktide Harry fixed him with an unblinking stare. "That is none of my concern. Whoever it was, I am sure they have received it loud and clear, and they will take the appropriate actions. Meanwhile, Magistrate Inspector, you and your boys have cleaned up my docks. And so life moves ever forward."

"Not yet, it doesn't," Dax said. "I mean to find justice for her."

Blacktide Harry leaned forward in his throne of crates. "Nothing in the rules about justice, Inspector. Your job here is to tidy things up. Clean up the mess that someone made. Whoever that message was intended for? Let them do their business."

"That message was once a person, and finding out what happened to her is exactly my job, Harry. And I do not intend to leave Prionside till I have accomplished it."

Blacktide Harry pursed his lips and looked Dax up and down with cold, unblinking eyes. Despite his convictions, Dax wondered if he had overstepped. But the Blacktide merely shook his head. "You've grown up a bit from that lost little pup that used to chase our Alys around."

"Yes, I suppose I have." Dax took a step forward and the skiff rocked a bit. "The girl was Lydia Ashdown." He saw the recognition in Blacktide Harry's eyes. "I have no doubt that her family will be eternally grateful to any who would bring justice to their daughter and their family name."

The Blacktide smirked, his teeth sharp and white beneath the black of his mustache. "And here I thought you were a crusader, Inspector. But clearly this would be quite a feather in your cap."

"Not mine, Harry. Yours. If you give us free rein in Prionside until this matter is done, I will be sure your name is brought to the attention of Lord Ashdown himself. Discreetly, of course."

There was a long, tension-filled silence, made all the more profound given the amount of rough men and women who lined the walls and walkways. Then, suddenly, the Blacktide began to laugh. The sound was rough and barking. "You've been teaching him well," he said through his laughter.

"Who thought he was actually listening?" Alys remarked.

The Blacktide chucked a few more times. "Blacktide Harry, friend of the noble houses," he said. "I find I do like the ring of that. Very well, Inspector, you and my dear Alys have my permission to poke your nose under every rock in this district. But I cannot guarantee what you might find hiding under those rocks," he added menacingly. "Since your success might even benefit me now, I have something that might get you started."

A scrawny, rough-looking man with the stylized hook and rat tattoo of the Stevedore Rats on the side of his neck came down the scaffold. "I's seen the twist earlier," he said with a vigorous nod. "Had a black cloak on, skulking around like she up to no good." He laughed at what Dax assumed was his brilliantly ironic statement, and around the room, other harsh laughter came back.

Alys put a hand up and gave Dax a sharp look indicating he should let her do the talking. She stepped to the bow of the skiff.

"Not everyone can be as respectable as you, Master Hookworm," Alys said with a mocking bow, and the coarse crowd erupted in laughter once more. "But thankfully your keen abilities for detection saw through her subterfuge, so why don't you tell me where you saw her?"

The Rat leaned forward, his hands gripping the walkway, and he leered down at Alys. "The Blacktide says the information is mine, broker. Information is your trade. You want mine, you offer me a deal, sweet-like, then, maybe I'll tell you what I saw," he said as the other Stevedore Rats around on the scaffolding laughed and cheered him on.

Alys locked eyes with the man, and her lips peeled back into a cruel grin. "Oh dear Master Hookworm. A deal, you say? Well then, here is my offer. I offer silence, Hookworm," she said, her voice shifting from the playful lightness of her previous conversation to a cold, edged tone. "I offer my continued silence, Hookworm, about that night with you and the bucket of fish," she said.

Hookworm reacted as if she had stuck him in the nethers with a sharpened blade.

"T—Tigress," Hookworm stammered out. "Saw her going to the Tigress!"

"You're sure?"

"That's where she went when I spied her. It was just before sundown. I swear it!"

Alys gave him a gentle smile. "I thank you, Master Hookworm." She gave a deep bow to the Blacktide, then turned to Dax. "Get us moving."

Dax moved to the other side of the skiff and began to pole them away, back down the canal and out of the Sumpworks.

"Lot of brass in there, Dax. Bartering with the Blacktide."

"It worked," Dax said.

"It did," Alys replied. "It also could have gotten us both killed. Next time, you let me do the talking. That's why you're paying me."

He nodded and gave her a small smile. "Master Hookworm looked quite surprised."

Alys's expression softened and she grinned back. "He most certainly did."

Poling the skiff through the dark tunnel, the two were quiet for a moment. "I don't suppose you're going to tell me what happened with him and the bucket of fish?" Dax said.

Alys settled back onto the floor of the skiff. "Sure," she said with a smile. "But not for free."

Act 3
The Lady or the Tiger

The mist had grown heavier, like a drizzle that did not fall so much as lie upon the very air itself. Alys walked down the street, her boot heels making a sharp rhythm in the muffled air. As she walked, she methodically cracked each knuckle on her first hand, and then the other before starting over again.

The Tigress, she thought. *The thrice-damned Tigress.*

"That thing is almost as big as you are."

Alys was so caught up in her own thoughts that she barely heard Dax when he spoke. "What?" she asked.

He gestured with a finger toward the large scythe across her back. "That monstrosity. You didn't have it back when we..." he paused. "The last time I saw you."

"Oh," Alys said. "My Aunty. Well, you see, Inspector, in a fight, it's the blade you don't see that is the one that'll be your gasper. So while everyone is so focused on what Aunty is up to..." She gestured down to the twin daggers hanging from her belt. "They don't see these."

As Dax's eyes tracked down, she let the weighted end of the garrote drop from her sleeve and in a blur, it was up and wrapped around the Inspector's throat. "And they surely don't see this," she said drawing him closer till her face was mere inches away from his.

"Cute," Dax said, slowly sliding a finger up between the thin wire and the exposed flesh of his collar.

"Aren't I though?" she said, releasing the tension and allowing the garrote to slip free.

She moved ahead of him, not quite willing to allow herself to walk at his side. Her hand trailed over the stones of the buildings as she walked, feeling the contours of the carved images under her fingertips. Highside might have the beautiful marble statues of the First Ascended, but the simple relief carvings on every Lowside building always felt more right to her.

"So are you going to tell me what's bothering you?" Dax asked. "It's making me nervous."

His tone was light, but there was enough underneath to show he was not totally unaware of her shift in mood. She bristled at having her discomfort called out so easily, but she wasn't surprised. He had always been better at reading people than she gave him credit for.

Especially her.

Of course, that went both ways. Since she had seen him on the docks, it had been apparent there was something Dax was withholding.

"I'm not crazy about going to brothels," she said with a shrug.

"A what? A brothel? What would Lydia be doing in a Prionside brothel?"

"Why do most people go to brothels?"

He wrinkled his lip. "You don't believe Lydia Ashdown was paying for... ahem... well, you know, any more than I do."

"You said she was seeing someone her parents didn't approve of. And I didn't say she was paying for it."

That seemed to give him pause. He had his thinking frown on, she noticed. "Do you think it was love?" he asked. "That perhaps she fell in love with someone from the Tigress?"

Oh, Dax. Always the idealist. There was a time when Alys had loved that about him, but that was when they had been childish and foolish and weak. Alys wasn't any of those things anymore.

"Look. I'm not doubting the power of a Highside bleeding heart, but let me tell you how it works in Lowside." She gestured to the streets around them, the mud and cobbles, refuse-filled gutters, and tightly-packed stone and wood buildings.

"You grow up down here, you don't dream of true love. You dream of opportunity. So, you see a Highside toff making time with a Lowsider, that's not a love story for the troubadours. That's a mark about to be skinned." She offered him a conciliatory shrug. "So, no, I don't think it was love, Dax. I think she was being conned."

"I see your opinion of people is as low as it always was."

"When you meet the Tigress, you'll understand why."

"I thought the Tigress was a brothel."

"The Tigress is both place and person, and the world would be a damn sight better if both were burned to the ground and someone pissed on the ashes," Alys said in an even voice.

Dax grimaced. "Charming."

"Oh, the place oozes charm. Like an open sore. Speaking of which, I suppose I should recommend you not avail yourselves of the services of the house."

"But I was hoping they might offer breakfast," he said with a disappointed sigh.

"Humor, Magistrate Inspector? Well done, but since we've arrived at our destination, perhaps it is time for you to reassume your customary mantle of serious, sullen bastard."

She gestured up above her head. A worn wooden sign swung in the wind. The sign itself had been crudely shaped and painted to look like a roaring tiger with a nude woman astride the back, but the paint was so faded and worn that the only remaining bits of color were dark black stripes.

Alys walked up the two steps and stood in front of the door made from thick wood and reinforced with rusted iron bands. She rapped twice on the door. A small panel opened, revealing an eye and part of a scarred face. The eye roved over Alys.

"Hello, Raff," Alys said, giving her sweetest smile to the scarred visage in the peephole.

The small panel slammed shut. A moment later, the sharp sounds of bolts being thrown back sounded and the heavy door swung open. Inside, was a massive man, his bald head and face heavily scarred and the lid of his left eye hanging limply down. He nodded his immense head in Alys's direction, but it was hard to see where the movement originated from, as he seemed to possess no discernible neck.

Alys rested a hand on one of his immense forearms. "Squinting Raff, allow me to introduce Magistrate Inspector Daxton Ellis."

"Another magistrate," Squinting Raff growled. "Place is lousy with them this week, and the last one didn't even pay fully." He towered over Dax and pushed a finger the size of a blood sausage into Dax's chest. "You pay yours upfront, gray-bars," he growled. "New house policy, thanks to your friend skipping on the doxy's due."

Dax's face showed utter shock, though Alys couldn't tell which had ruffled him more: being accosted by the mountain of flesh that was Squinting Raff, or that he was not the first magistrate to visit the Tigress of late.

Alys grabbed his arm and pulled him away from the guard. Pushing aside the heavy velvet curtains, she escorted Dax into the heart of the Tigress.

Inside, the parlor was lush and decadent. Light shone behind colored glass coverings, causing a fantastic array of colors to cover the space. Rugs with gaudy and intricate designs covered the floor. On chairs and divans across the room rested men and women in outfits that were as ridiculous as they were revealing. They were meant to appear tantalizing and seductive, but Alys had long ago stopped looking only at the bodies and clothing. Now, all she could focus on were the eyes. Sunken. Hollow. Desperate.

She loathed this place.

As she and Dax entered, all eyes were upon them, and as soon as they seemed to recognize Alys, they were off their seats, pressing around her.

"Alys, got something juicy for you. Won't cost you much," said one woman.

A young man tried to catch her eye. Gold, she thought might be his name, but she wasn't sure. It had been a while since she was last here and it was so damned hard to keep up. "I've got drops on the Gray Needle bunch. Good. Valuable," he said, but Alys shook her head.

"Got dirt on a Highside toff, Sewall his name was. Good dirt, Alys!" a girl named Genna said, reaching out toward her.

"Alys!"

"Dirt!"

"Won't cost you much."

But Alys wasn't listening. This was part of the reason she hated coming to a brothel. Every whore had information to sell, but usually it was shit. Exaggerated and twisted to make it seem richer, juicier, and worth more money. Even off their backs, they couldn't stop deceiving.

"I'm not fishing tonight," Alys said, raising her voice a bit to be heard over the clamor. "I'm looking for one piece. Highside twist. More lamb than mutton. Came by earlier in the night. So who's got something juicy now?"

At her words, the crowd of prostitutes grew quieter, and before she had finished speaking, they were already slinking back to their seats. From the upstairs landing, she heard a woman clear her throat. When the affected tones of that nasally voice came, Alys understood why the whores had all gone quiet. Her teeth clenched.

"Why, dear little Rose, how good to see you."

Alys raised her eyes to the landing. At the top of the staircase was a woman in a long dress and a fur mantle draped over her shoulders. She was the epitome of faded, wilted elegance. The once-beautiful face was caked with heavy powder and brightly colored rouge on her cheeks. Her lips were painted with a spot of vibrant red in the very middle, giving them a perpetual pout that was intended to make her look young and coquettish, but instead made her look sour.

The Tigress.

Alys took a step back. "You forget, Tigress. It's Alys," she said, keeping her voice even. "Not Rose. Alys."

The Tigress, wafted a hand dismissively in the air and batted her heavily colored eyes. "Of course, dear. It is just so hard to keep track of the little, insignificant details."

It was an easy shot. A cheap shot. But, as always with the Tigress, it wasn't the opening shot to worry about. That would be the knife she slipped in when you were distracted.

Despite knowing better, Alys felt the words coming to her mouth almost unbidden. "Of course," she said with a sweet smile.

"Totally understandable. They say the first thing to go with age is the memory." That was a cheap shot too, she had to admit. For a flash of a moment, she felt a little ashamed at reaching for such low-hanging fruit, but when she saw the lines around the Tigress's eyes tighten she couldn't help adding, "Or is it the looks?"

The Tigress began to come down the wooden steps. "From what I have observed among the more aged of our clientèle, it is the sense of whimsy that leaves first. As the years go by, there are so few surprises left in the world." She paused on the last of the steps and let her heavy-lidded gaze fall upon Dax. "And yet, there can still be a shock or two left."

She grinned and Alys felt the cold tension in her stomach tighten even more. There was the Tigress's knife, aimed squarely at Alys's weakest point.

Dax.

"My little pets," the Tigress said, clapping her hands. Immediately, every whore in the room sat up straight, attentive as a child at lessons, their unwavering attention on the Tigress. "Why it seems we are blessed this evening." She walked to Dax and trailed her hand across the cloth of his gray, magistrate's coat. "This is young master Daxton Ellis, son to the High Chancellor himself."

In perfect choreography, every whore in the room prostrated themselves at the name. There was a breathy, whispered chorus of honorifics as each whispered "My lord."

Even postured, Alys saw the look in their eyes. Saw desire and hunger not born of lust, but opportunity.

Dax's face showed his surprise. "You know me, madam?"

"Oh, everyone knows you, my dear. Or they know your story, at least," the Tigress intoned. "The little orphan girl who thought she could rise to the station of a noble. And not just any noble

23

house, mind you, but the trueborn line of Aedan himself. How is your uncle, the king?"

Even from across the room, Alys saw Dax's face grow pale, and he froze in place. Alys shook her head, trying to break the old madam's control of the room. "You going to waste time with history, Tigress? When there is business to be done?"

The Tigress locked eyes with her. "But it is so fascinating a history, my dear girl. You cannot deny my little darlings their entertainment." Her eyes gleamed behind the garish make-up and skewered Alys with her gaze. "You must let them fawn and have some small amount of fun with him, dear. They will likely never get to be so near such a bright star as this again. And don't you worry. Thanks to you, they already know what happens if they get too close."

Alys glared back, but as angry as she was, Dax seemed more furious. His jaw was clenched hard enough that the muscles in his neck stood out. And she was not the only one who had picked up on it. Squinting Raff was easing behind Dax, a hand already on his blade in the event there was to be trouble.

She wasn't happy about it but she choked back her anger. The Tigress would get hers one day. Just not today.

"Fair cop, Tigress. You've made your point."

"What point is that, dear?"

Alys ducked her chin. "Your house. Your rules."

"Indeed," the Tigress replied, sauntering to one of the couches to distractedly stroke the hair of one of the young men, before pushing him away. "So, perhaps you can explain what brings you and the dear magistrate inspector to my house at this unholy hour," she said to Alys as she walked over.

Alys's nose filled with the scent of her, cloying and overpowering. Rosewater and lavender and spice-chew. It made the bile rise in the back of Alys's throat. "There was a dead girl found down at the docks. Highborn. She came here before that."

The Tigress looked at Alys with her heavy-lidded eyes and an expression of utter boredom. "And?"

"What can you tell us about her then?" Dax asked, seemingly recovered enough from his shock and anger to speak out.

"Well, that of course depends on what you are willing to pay. Tell me, Magistrate Inspector, what is the little slattern worth to you?"

Dax drew himself tall and straight. "That girl was a Lady of a noble house and family."

The Tigress laughed, a sound that ranged uncomfortably between sultry and mocking. "Oh, believe me, Inspector. I am quite familiar with Lydia Ashdown."

Dax stepped forcefully toward the Tigress, closing the distance till he was staring into her face. Immediately, Alys had a blade near her hand. Behind her, she felt Squinting Raff step into the room with a heavy menacing tread.

The Tigress held out a hand in the direction of her bouncer as the whores held their collective breath.

"Tell me what you know," Dax said, his voice low.

The older woman seemed unfazed by his aggressive posturing, though. A pink tongue darted out and licked the crimson of her red lips as the Tigress made a low noise in her throat. "Ooh, Inspector. Forceful and menacing. Your father would approve."

She raised her painted nails, studied them for a moment, and put her hand against his chest once more. This time, the Tigress slowly pushed Dax away. "But it is a pointless display. Surely she has told you the rules. There is nothing for free in Lowside. Not even for you, young Lord Ellis."

Alys reached into an inner pocket and pulled out two pressed gold sovereigns. She held them up and then made them dance across her knuckles. "Two," she said.

"Four," the Tigress countered. She rolled her eyes at Dax. "You know he can afford it, dear."

Gritting her teeth hard enough to feel them grinding in to dust, Alys pulled out two more of the valuable coins. The Tigress extended her hand and Alys dropped them into her palm. She was careful not to let her skin touch the Tigress's. The river water and ocean smell of the Sumpworks would wash off, but the taint of the Tigress was more than Alys was willing to deal with tonight.

Adjusting her fur robe, the Tigress sighed heavily. "Young Lydia came to my door looking for employment, actually. She claimed she needed money. Desperately and urgently." She shook her head with an almost-convincing air of sympathy. "She must have been running from something dark, the poor girl."

"Dark enough to turn to whoring?" Alys asked.

The Tigress regarded her with heavily lined eyes. "It is not an uncommon tale."

"What was she running from?" Dax asked.

"I am sure I do not know, but I am not the person you should be directing your questions to regarding young Lydia's dilemmas. You would be best served finding a young man named Calder. He is an inkman in this district."

"Inkman?" Dax asked. "A tattooist? Who is he? Where can we find him?"

Inwardly, Alys groaned. Too eager. Much too eager.

"The district is so busy these days, my lovely man. So many names and faces to be expected to keep track of one individual."

Even before the Tigress had finished her words, Dax pulled forth a stack of gleaming coins. "I want to know about Calder," he said, his voice hard.

A wrinkled hand snatched the coins and made them into the folds of the Tigress's dressing gown with such smooth ease that even Alys had a hard time following the motion.

The Tigress sighed theatrically. "Alas, poor Calder's talent was not as great as his capacity for misfortune. A degenerate gambler from what I have known. His predilection has cost him a place in a number of crews. It is this young man who Lydia has been sharing time with for the last few months." The Tigress shook her head. "Such a naive little girl, falling for such a one as him. Calder owed many things to many people. Find him, and perhaps he will have your answers."

Alys had a sour taste in her mouth, though whether it was from her proximity to the Tigress or from the picture beginning to form she did not know. Calder the inkman seemed like one of a thousand Lowside shits and he had likely seen Little Miss Highside coming like a torch in the night.

Dax spoke again. "Where is he?"

The Tigress slowly opened her dressing gown and one of the gold coins appeared back in her hand. She slid the gold coin down across the wrinkled skin of her cleavage till it was out of sight. Then, she cast her eyes in Dax's direction. "My part is done, Inspector. Finding him is your task."

Alys moved over to Dax's side and took his arm in a firm grip. "We should go. Miserable experience as always, Tigress," she said, nodding in the older woman's direction.

The Tigress drew her fur mantle closer around her. "Truly," she said back. "It is so memorable when you show up at my door. It is like a dose of the pox." She batted her eyes at Dax, and let a bit of the mantle fall, exposing a bare shoulder. "Best of luck to you, Inspector," she said. "And should you see your father, send him my regards."

Squinting Raff escorted them back onto the street. Alys could still smell the sickly sweet scent of the Tigress's perfume on her clothes and in her hair. It made her want to jump into the Prion's dark waters. She glanced over to Dax. His brow was creased with thought.

When they were out of sight of the Tigress's domain, Dax frowned, but in his eyes gleamed renewed determination. "Well," he said. "We have some progress."

Surprised, Alys stopped walking and turned toward him. "We almost had a lot worse. What was the righteous, angry magistrate act in there?" she said. "You know Squinting Raff could have had you in a moment."

Dax shrugged. "I assumed you had me covered on that front."

"Awfully big assumption."

"It didn't used to be," she thought she heard him say, but before she could be sure Dax was already moving on. "So we know who she was seeing. Now we just have to find him. Where would he be?"

"Probably far away from here."

"Do you know any way to track down somebody like that?"

Alys crossed her arms over her chest. "Do you think I can just mine some connections and find any degenerate that happens to be Lowside?"

"Can you?"

"Of course I can, but what's the point, Dax?" she said. Seeing that the light was not fading from his eyes, she shook her head. "Look, the guy is likely a clipper looking for an easy score. As soon as his pigeon wound up dead, he likely went underground to lay low."

"What do you mean?"

28

"She was a mark. This Calder went after her, got what he needed, and then either got her involved in something that got her killed or killed her himself."

"Ever the cynic, Alys. How can you assume he was just using her? What if he did love her? And she, him?"

Alys scoffed, but frustration gave an edge to her words. "You always did love a good fairy tale, Dax. You just could never let it go."

He opened his mouth as if to retort, but then seemingly thought better of it. "Either way," he said, the words sharp and clipped, "this investigation is not over until we find Calder. If you think you can do it."

Alys laughed at that. Trying to goad her into it. It was so clumsy it was almost endearing. "You want the inkman, Inspector? I'll get you your inkman."

Act 4
The Course of True Love

It wasn't even dark by the time Alys had tracked him down.

The more that Alys asked around, the more she was able to get a picture of her quarry. In addition to being a fairly skilled hand with a tapping needle and ink, Master Calder was also a degenerate gambler.

He was in deep to a number of folks all over the district. Supposedly, some of Keyburn's boys out of the Olde Sportsman's Hall had stumbled across him sometime last night. No one had seen him on the street since then, which meant he'd still be at the Sportsman's. If he was still alive, of course.

It had been a few months since she had had occasion to visit the place, but things had not changed. At this point in the afternoon, things were quiet, with just a few men and women sitting at the tables dealing King's Cross, or rolling dice.

Most noticeably though, the rat pit was empty and silent. In the center of the room were rows of wooden benches set in an amphitheater-style around a low circular wall. Inside the wall, sawdust lined the wooden floor to make clean-up easier, but the room still smelled like old blood and animal fear.

Behind the bar, Magda was there, as always, wiping down the polished wood with a rag. She pushed back her blonde curls from her face and reached for two small jacks. She poured them each a dram from the jug of punch on the counter.

"Ta, Magda," Alys said in thanks, knocking back the drink and feeling the burn down her throat. Dax followed suit.

"Not at all, Alys," Magda said. "Heard you been to see the Tigress of late. Figured you could use a dose of stability." She glanced down over at Dax. "Especially given your escort."

"Business has its strange demands some days, Magda. Keyburn here?"

"Out round the back. Dealing with a delinquent collection. But go on with you. He'll be glad to see you, busy or not."

"Cheers, Magda," Alys said, motioning for Dax to follow.

"Glad for the sight of you, Alys," Magda called after them.

Alys stepped out into the late afternoon daylight. The smell coming from the small sty of pigs kept behind the building was sharp and pungent, and the animals themselves were loud. Even over the sound of pigs, Alys heard the heavy slapping sounds of someone getting the worst of a beating.

Dax's hand went to the hilt of his sword, but her hand shot out and caught his wrist tightly. Her eyes met his, and she shook her head. He frowned, but released his grip.

Alys walked around the side of the big building. There, behind the pig pen, two men were taking turns methodically beating a third man. A tall man with thick, dark sideburns and a long face leaned against the wall. He looked decidedly bored with the proceedings.

"Running a successful business can be so tedious, can't it, Keyburn?" Alys called out.

The tall man's eyes widened. "Alys!" he said jovially, leaping off the wall and coming toward them. He wrapped Alys in a tight embrace and grinned at Dax. "And you bring a guest as well." He bowed low. "Keyburn the Sportsman. You must be the Magistrate Inspector. The Blacktide sent word you'd be out and about the district."

A heavy smacking sound came from behind Keyburn, followed by a groan of pain. Alys peered around Keyburn's shoulder. "Sorry to interrupt you, Key, but I was hoping you might have a line on someone I'm trying to track down."

"Please. You are never an interruption, Alys. The boys could do with a bit of a break." He whistled once, sharply, and the two large men let the beaten man fall heavily to the ground, where he lay panting and bleeding.

Keyburn turned back to Alys. "Now, what is it I can do for you, fair cousin?"

Alys smiled. "I'm looking for a Lowside slummer. Inkman. Between crews, likely. Gambler and grafter named Calder."

There was a muffled moan from the man on the ground.

"Why young master Calder is right here," Keyburn said, stepping back and gesturing to the man on the ground. "We were just discussing the negatives inherent in not only being delinquent in repaying a debt, but also dishonesty."

Keyburn walked over to Calder and gave the man a quick sharp kick to the ribs. "He assured me he would have my money as of two days ago. And yet, when the lads came across him last night, he was empty-handed. Tsk tsk."

At his feet, Calder moaned and rolled over onto his back, breathing hard.

Alys looked over to Dax. His lips were set in a tight line. He had not taken his eyes off Calder since Keyburn had confirmed his identity. She could practically hear his teeth grinding together.

She sighed.

"How deep is he in to you, Key?" she asked.

"Including the juice on his original borrow?" he said. "Twelve stacks."

Alys's mouth fell open. "Twelve stacks?" she said, shooting a look at the man on the ground. "You must be a complete degenerate to rack up numbers like that." Alys rubbed a hand over her forehead in frustration and sighed once more. "Look, Key. I got need for him. You willing to sell me his marker?"

Keyburn seemed a bit surprised, but he slowly nodded his head. "I would be, but I gotta warn you, cousin. He likely owes at least one other house besides mine. A few toughs came asking for him early this morning. I had to remind them that I had found him first, so I had first claim." Keyburn shrugged. "If you buy up his marker, you won't be the only one with a claim on him." He smiled at her with stained teeth. "Never let it be said I entered into a deal without giving full disclosure."

"I am obliged, Key, and I'll take my chances." She looked down at the form slumped on the ground. "I do need him to talk, though. You started work on his teeth yet?"

"Not at all," Key said. "Just a bit of the body for today. Was thinking ear tomorrow, then perhaps teeth, but not my problem anymore. Provided you have something worth his twelve stacks, Alys."

"I know the names of the Razors that three of the schools are putting up to fight in the tournament next month. Not the bloodsport down by the gate, mind you. The big, sanctioned fights up near Crucis. That worth something to you?"

Keyburn's eyes lit up. "Why yes, that would be a fine start on the marker."

"Then we'll call it that, and two more pieces of substance, if and when they cross my path." She pressed her hand against her heart and then held her hand out toward Keyburn.

Looking at her outstretched hand for a moment, Keyburn sighed and pressed his own palm against his heart and took her by the forearm. "I always did have a soft spot for you, Alys." He smiled though. "Well, at least I know that unlike with Master Calder here, you are good for your promised payment."

"Of course. Your Razors are Coraxon Nox, a Vertigo, Vestan, an Aegis, and from Faith, new face named Gideon. The Faith is a lock to win it all. Trust me."

"Your word has always been good enough," Keyburn said. "My thanks, Alys." He glanced back to Calder. "I fear I may have gotten the better of you on this deal, cousin," he said. "Feel free to take your new friend inside the Olde Sport. Drinks on me, and a place for you to talk."

"Ta, Key. Much gratitude."

"Come!" Keyburn said. "Enough sun and dust. Time for healthy darkness and drink." With that, he headed back toward the Hall.

Alys followed Keyburn, leaving Dax to bear the burden of the beaten Calder.

Inside, she selected a comfortable booth in the rear corner of the building. Dax dropped Calder unceremoniously onto the carved wooden bench, and the young man slumped down in the seat. He tried to raise his head and look at the two of them, but both his eyes had started to swell shut. His exposed skin was a colorful mixture of red blood and dark ink from the designs that covered him.

The knuckles of his fingers were marked, and Alys recognized a few of the designs there. A rose blooming from the hilt of a dagger. He had come of age in a crew. This one started young. On the back of the hand was a crown wrapped in chains. She counted four links. Imprisoned four times. It was a wonder Dax didn't recognize him, the little idiot had been down in the depths of the House of Law enough times.

Alys shook her head. She had just purchased a very expensive piece of shit.

Dax cleared his throat. "I am Magistrate Inspector Daxton Ellis. I was told you knew Lydia Ashdown. She was found dead on the docks here in Prionside early this—"

"I done it," Calder said, staring with ravaged, swollen eyes. "I killed her. Take me in."

Dax stopped dead in his words. "What did you say?" he said quietly.

"Ah, a Lowside love story," Alys said. "She surely fell for the right man. A few words, a couple of lovely promises, and then murdered and left on a Prionside dock."

"Just... just take me in," Calder said.

Without warning, Dax grabbed Calder and lifted him up in his seat. "You don't get to issue orders here, you shit," he hissed. "Lydia. I want to know why. Why!"

"Dax," Alys said, and the sound of her voice seemed to cut through his rage. He blinked once, and then released Calder, letting the man fall heavily back down into his chair.

Alys moved in close. "I own your marker. I now own you. So, the Inspector wants the sordid tale, and I mean for him to have it. So, you speak. Did she wise up to your grift? Is that what happened?"

Calder blinked once. "I ain't never had anything good in my life. I ain't saying that to make excuses. It's just... just bad luck. Bad damned luck." He seemed to catch himself then, stopping his words and looking past Dax to the few other customers sitting in the dark corners of the Sportsman's. "She was just a mark," Calder said. "I was trying to make some easy coin, and I played her for a while but she wised up, and I..."

He stopped looking at the other customers and returned his attention first to Alys and then to Dax. "I'll make a full confession. Anything you want. But at the station. Not here. Out of Lowside. There ain't anything left for me here now," he said before beginning to weep.

Dax was quiet for a long moment before he stood up and headed to the bar.

Alys sat down beside him as he ordered a drink from Magda and drained it silently. "That's it then. It's over. As simple as that." He looked at her. "You going to say I told you so?"

"Thought it would be tacky."

Dax offered a weak smile, but it faded as his eyes went back to Calder. "Just didn't think it'd actually turn out like this. It's so simple. Girl meets the wrong guy and gets killed for it."

"Almost. Girl falls in love with the wrong guy and gets killed for it."

There was a long pause until, finally, Alys couldn't take it. "Why are you looking so glum. It's not like you killed the girl." She caught Dax's eye. "You did good. Your chief magistrate will be thrilled. You found the killer. Got your precious justice."

Dax's brow remained furrowed and she saw the tension in his clenched jaw. "I didn't kill her," he said, his eyes closed tightly, "but maybe I could've saved her."

Alys was quiet, unsure what to say, and unwilling to interrupt him now that he was finally bringing out into the open whatever had been cutting at him all day.

He drew in a long, shuddering breath. "Three months ago, when Kara Ashdown came to me and asked me to look for her sister, I looked. And fairly quickly, everything in Highside was coming up empty. Not just the usual quiet of discretion and secrecy to protect delicate reputations. There was nothing of Lydia up there. And I knew, knew in my gut, that she had gone Lowside."

He looked at her then, and she saw the pain and shame and disappointment in his eyes, and she remembered the last time he had looked like that. Only this time, those feelings were directed at himself instead of at her.

"I didn't look," Dax said. "Not even a single inquiry. I didn't want to get near Lowside. I couldn't." Dax shook his head. "At first, I thought it was because of you. Because I was afraid to see you. Even this morning on the dock, it was all I could think of. Seeing you again. But just now, with Calder... I realized it was really something more."

Suddenly, it clicked for Alys. "You wanted to believe the fairy tale," she said softly. "You wanted them to have been in love and run off together and be living somewhere happier ever after."

Dax's silence showed that she had hit the target.

"Then you're just as big an idiot today as you were then."

"Maybe I am," Dax muttered before downing the rest of his drink in a quick, savage gulp. "Come on. I've got a prisoner to transport, and the sooner I'm out of Lowside the better."

**

Alys noticed their first tail as soon as they left the Sportsman's.

He was good. Not great, but not an amateur. Alys picked him up anyway, almost right away. The second one was not nearly as talented. She spotted him even before he committed to moving after them.

Dax had Calder a half step in front of him, but he leaned his head toward her. "We're being followed."

"I know."

"How many?"

As three men stepped out from the corner ahead, Alys sighed. "Enough."

Three to the front, and three to the back. Not good. Alys recognized the man who led the trio at the front: Festa. A Razor for hire around Lowside and lead dog in a wolf-pack known as the Leather Aprons. Worst of the worst.

Calder caught sight of the men ahead and began whimpering.

"Six of them," Dax said in a low voice.

"Five and the Razor," she said, pointing to the big man walking in the lead.

Dax blew out a low breath. "If he gets his power—"

"Then we don't let him get a chance," she said, cutting Dax off. "Worry not, darling Dax. I will take care of the big bad Razor."

The six men closed in. "We were just coming for the boy," Festa said. "Had no direct mention of you, Alys, nor your friend. But now..." He shrugged.

Alys nodded. "We play the dice as they roll, yeah?"

The Razor slowly advanced across the cobblestones of the street. The men behind them spread out, ensuring there was no way past them.

"Try not to get yourself killed before you pay me, Dax," Alys said.

Then, without warning, she whipped a blade through the air aimed directly at the face of the Razor and followed immediately by a small sack. With both airborne, Alys charged.

The Razor's face shifted into a confident smile, and she felt the tell-tale pressure against her chest as the big man touched the strange power that made Razors so formidable. In a blinding flash, he swept his blade from its sheath and deflected her thrown blade. Knocking away the weapon with an almost nonchalant motion, he reversed his blade to block the small sack.

Now, it was Alys's turn to grin. As Festa struck the bag, it exploded in a cloud of flour, pepper, and ground glass, covering the man's face. That was the great thing about Razors. They were so used to being so much better than everyone else that they forgot how to cheat.

Immediately, she felt the pressure from the build-up of his power falter and fade as he clutched at his eyes. Closing the distance, Alys struck him across the jaw with the knuckle dusters on her left hand. She felt the jaw shatter under the blow.

Following up the strike, she pounced, her weight bearing him down to the street. He thrashed as they hit the ground, but she had already pulled one of her blades. She thrust it into his side over and over as he spasmed.

Leaving the big Razor on the ground to bleed out, she came up and threw her blood-stained blade into the chest of one of the toughs approaching her, knocking him from his feet.

Dax traded blows with two more of the fighters, swinging his sword and a metal truncheon. He seemed to be holding his own.

From the corner of her eye, Alys saw one of the Leather Aprons coming up behind Dax. She darted over and slipped the garrote around his neck, holding him close as he kicked and struggled. Over his shoulder, she caught sight of one of the men dragging Calder down a side alley as he screamed.

As she let the man's body fall to the ground, Alys saw Dax standing over the bodies of the two he had engaged with. He was breathing a bit hard, and had a few small cuts across his arms.

Looking around, his eyes grew wild. "Where's Calder?"

Alys gestured in the direction of the alley. "Gone. Taken."

"Taken?" Dax said. "Why the hell take him?" He sprinted over to the alley and cursed, leaning against the wall to catch his breath. "Money? Keyburn said there were others that he owed."

Alys stared down at the body at her feet. "That Razor knew me. He should have known we had the Blacktide's blessing, yet he was willing to cross me and Harry both, without hesitation."

"You know who they are?"

"Recognized the Razor at the front. They're Leather Aprons." She spat onto one of the bodies at her feet. "Bad people."

"You know where to find them?"

Alys started walking. "I know where they are and they're not going to see me coming."

ACT 5
SLAUGHTERHOUSE CONFESSIONAL

Dax followed Alys over the Prionside rooftops.

He made an incautious step and the old building's crumbling stone moved under his foot. Dax lurched forward, dropping to his knees hard and clinging to the roof's thatch. It was far enough down that he did not want to consider what would happen if he fell from this height.

Alys stood over him, shaking her head. She raised a single finger to her lips.

Dax felt the heat of embarrassment on his cheeks, but worked his way to his feet. Alys was moving on, her steps light and sure as she nimbly made her way across the long roof. Dax followed as best he could.

Lifting himself to peer over the edge, Dax saw a huge corral filled with hogs before a large, run-down stone building. Parts of the furthest wall had crumbled into the river long ago. The sharp wind shifted and the full stench of the hog pens hit him. It was a choking, noxious odor. A reek of shit and fear and blood. He put his forearm over his face to keep from breathing it in.

Alys nodded. "The Leather Aprons are butchers," she said. "Pig or person, makes not a whit of difference to them. Long as they get to cut."

Dax took slow breaths through his mouth. "Calder?"

"If they wanted him dead, they would have gutted him back outside the Sportsman's. The fact that they didn't means he's likely alive. So there is that. The other thing we have going for us is that they won't expect us to come after him."

She pulled out a small iron hook and wedged it tightly between two large stone pieces, then handed him a piece of leather with copper teeth sewn into it. "Wrap that around your hand, leaving the teeth exposed on the outside. They should be right across the center of your palm. Grip tight to slow yourself." She pulled out a thin coil of rope, attached one end to the iron hook, and went over the side.

She gracefully made her way down the tall stone face of the building, the thin rope unspooling behind her. Then, she ducked into the shadows across from the Leather Aprons's slaughterhouse.

Before he could lose more of his nerve, Dax wrapped the leather strap around his right hand and dropped over the edge. The rope slipped against the copper teeth as he plummeted the first few feet, but then he gripped hard and the teeth caught. Smoke from the friction seemed to rise from his palm as he descended, but it slowed him enough so he hit the ground with barely more than a slap of his boots on the causeway. He slipped into the hiding place beside Alys.

Her eyes were focused on the entrance to the slaughterhouse, but she held out her hand to him. For a brief moment, Dax almost took it with his own, but then he remembered the leather strap and passed that back to her.

"Still no movement over there. Usually there's be a few coming and going," she whispered.

"What is your plan?"

Alys bit her lip and pointed to the crumbling part of the building where the river lapped against the wreckage. "There. We go in that way, and we should be fairly blocked from sight until we're actually inside."

Slowly, they made their way down to the water's edge and Alys motioned him into the cold, murky water. As Dax slipped in and followed her along the docks, he did his best to keep his face above the waterline. The thought of the oily, brackish, black water going into his mouth kept his lips sealed tight.

Despite his discomfort, they crossed the remaining distance quickly, scrambling over the stones into the ramshackle rear of the building. The smell of the hogs was almost overpowering now, and yet above that, the unmistakable iron tang of blood filled the air.

He followed Alys cautiously, careful to place his feet exactly where she stepped as they made their way over rubble and into the building.

Alys froze.

Dax stopped where he was. The sound of his breathing seemed as loud as a shout, but over it he heard what caused Alys to stop: voices.

"I told you! I told you you'se cuttin too deep. Now he done nodded out again. What if we can't wake him up again? You wanna tell Lord Razorback we found him, but he ain't talkin no more?"

A second voice responded. It was full of bravado, but Dax caught the edge of uncertain fear. "Inkman ain't dead. Not yet, no way. Besides, we agreed. We find his rich twist before the rest of the skins, and we got it made. We bring her to Lord Razorback, we top cutters. Especially now that Festa is dirted."

In the shadows, Alys frowned. He responded in kind.

Suddenly, he heard one of the voices curse, and Dax tensed. His hand dropped to his blade, sure that they had been discovered, but Alys held a hand up, urging him to remain still.

"Shit! It's Gobber's pack. Back early and empty-handed, lazy sots," the first voice said urgently.

"Run out and meet him. Talk 'em and stall 'em like. I'll wake the inkman and get what we need before them others see what we got."

"Don't you kill him!"

"Tsh. If he tells me where the twist is, then we don't needs him no more. Now move!"

There was a sound of hurried footsteps from ahead of them, but Dax could not see anything to match with the sound. Alys slowly pulled out the garrote from within her sleeve and stretched it between her hands. "Wait here," she mouthed silently as she headed into the building's main area.

The moments passed like hours as Dax waited, his ears straining. He heard a slight shuffling noise, like boots sliding on the floor, then a soft thud. He held his breath.

"Dax!" he heard her whisper. "Get out here, now."

Dax broke from his hiding place and moved around the blind corridors. All around, the bodies of slaughtered hogs hung from iron hooks, dressed and open. The white of ribs shone against the bloody red of flesh.

In the center of the large room, tied fast to a chair, was Calder. Pooled around the young man's chair was a bright red puddle of blood.

Alys shook her head. "He is barely here. There is no way we can get him out of here. Just trying to lift him out of that chair and pieces of him are going to start falling off. Whatever you need from him, I suggest you get it now."

Dax frowned as he moved over to Calder. Kneeling in the sticky puddle of blood, he gently tried to rouse the young man. Blood covered Calder's face, and the dark red on the side of his head marked where his right ear had once been. His shirt was torn open, and his chest was streaked with blood. As Dax shook him, Calder's eyes began to flutter. Then, he came awake and began screaming.

Trying to quiet him, Dax held onto Calder's wrist, but the young man was hurt badly and his eyes rolled white with shock and fear. Before Dax could calm him, he heard a commotion toward the entrance.

Alys's voice cracked out to him, "On your feet, Dax." She wasn't whispering, and there was a sharp edge to her words that got his attention immediately. At the far end of the building, coming through the main entrance, were five rough-looking Leather Aprons.

"What the hell is this shit?" one of them said.

Alys reached behind her back and pulled the long scythe from its holder. She rapped the butt of the staff onto the ground and the long curving blade snapped into position with a menacing thrum. "This is doing things the hard way," she said, hoisting the scythe in her hands. "You with me, Inspector?"

Dax stood up from the puddle of Calder's blood and drew his long blade with a rasping sound of steel against leather. "Always," Dax said.

He charged forward, but Alys was already in motion, crossing the distance to the Leather Aprons in quick, darting steps. She reared back with the scythe as she ran and brought it around in a whistling arc. One of the toughs jumped back to avoid the huge curving blade, but another was not so lucky. He took the full force of the blow and it almost cut him in two. Even as she hit,

Alys pulled a dagger and threw it into the face of the man she had missed.

Dax caught one of the men as he brought his sword up to defend himself. Dax allowed his blade to strike against the Leather Apron's sword, but then kept charging forward, lowering his shoulder and sending him reeling. Dax took a step forward and kicked the man in the jaw. He felt bones give way under the blow.

The remaining two Leather Aprons turned and ran out the front entrance, scrambling in a frantic panic until they were gone from sight and Dax and Alys were alone with nothing but corpses.

"They're going to get reinforcements," Alys said, breathing hard.

As she spoke, Dax returned to the bloodied Calder. "Easy, boy," Dax said. "We're not going to let them hurt you anymore."

Calder's eyes flew open, wide with panic. He thrashed for a moment, but Dax felt how weak the man was. Alys was right; he wasn't going to make it out.

"Magistrate. You—you came for me?" the young man managed to stammer. His eyes grew wide and he gripped Dax's coat. "Lydia!" Calder gasped. "I love her. She deserves better. Better than me. Didn't tell them anything." Calder's eyes rolled wildly in his head as he began to fade once more.

Something clawed at Dax's awareness. He shook the dying boy, trying to get him to focus one last time. "What, Calder? What didn't you tell them?"

"Lydia's alive. You have to tell her. Tell her about me. Tell her I loved her." Blood welled up in from Calder's mouth and he choked on it. His eyes grew dimmer. "Better off without me," he whispered, and then the light went out in his eyes and Calder was gone.

"Lydia's alive? Calder?" Dax said, shaking the body. "Calder."

"He's gone," Alys said.

"Damn it," Dax said, sitting back. "He said Lydia's alive. But how? Where?"

Alys knelt in front of Calder's still form and pulled open his shirt. With the palm of her hand, she wiped away blood to expose a tattoo over his heart.

A tattoo in the shape of a sparrow.

Dax stared at the tattoo. It looked like the burn mark on Lydia's body. No, not like it. It was exactly the same.

"They faked it, Dax. I think he was telling the truth. Lydia Ashdown is still alive."

"But why? And where is she?"

"Only Lydia can tell us why." Alys stood up, wiping her bloody hands on her pant leg. "As to where, I have an idea, but I hope I'm wrong."

Act 6
The Best Laid Plans

As soon as Squinting Raff opened the door, Alys was already pushing it wider and storming inside. "Where's your boss? She's expecting me."

Raff stared at her for a moment and then jerked his chin upwards. "Her room," he growled. "You know the way."

Alys strode through the room in a flurry. The few whores still awake stirred as she crossed the space, but they kept them quiet and out of her way.

"You sure about this?" Dax asked as she reached the door.

"No," Alys said, but she rapped hard on the door.

There was a drawn out moment before the door opened, and there stood the Tigress. The make-up was thick on her face, and the casual dressing gown she wore was busy with a fur collar and gemstones. "My dear, what an unexpected pleasure. Your company twice in such a short interval. I am touched. Truly, I am."

Alys ignored the condescending tone. "I'm here to see Lydia."

The Tigress's eyes narrowed and she pursed her painted lips. "You've lost a step," the Tigress said, her hard green eyes glittering behind the heavy shadows of her make-up. "Or you're just getting soft."

Alys stepped inside the door, Dax following close behind. As he entered, the Tigress ran a wrinkled hand over his cheek. "I figured it was only a matter of time before I saw you in my bedchamber, Magistrate," she said with a throaty laugh.

Dax opened his mouth as if to say something, but stopped short. On the bed, amidst a sea of cushions, sat Lydia Ashdown.

The girl was a close match to the body on the docks, though the real Lydia here had larger eyes. They added to her look of desperate innocence as she sat up straight. "Daxton!" she exclaimed breathlessly. "The Lady of this house," she said, indicating the Tigress, "told me that you were searching for Calder. Tell me, I beg of you, have you found him?"

Dax took Lydia's hands as he knelt down before her. "Lydia! Three months your family has been searching for you. Kara was desperate with worry. This morning you were dead. What is going on?"

Lydia blinked her wide, round eyes and shuddered. "Lord Ellis, we had no choice. Things just got so out of hand so quickly, we had to find a way out. We had to!"

Dax shook his head emphatically. "But to fake your own deaths? To make even your family believe such a thing?" She began to tear up and Dax squeezed her hands. "What happened, Lydia?"

Lydia Ashdown took a deep breath. "When I met Calder, he was in a bad situation. But he was sweet and kind, and we..." Her words trailed off and her smile grew larger. "We fell in love. We wanted to leave, get out of Resa. Make a new life for ourselves out

52

in the Marches. You know my parents. And Calder, with everything...
It was a fresh start for both of us. Just the two of us."

"What happened?" Dax's voice was soft and gentle.

Lydia's face fell. "I did something foolish," she said quietly. "I
knew he owed much to his former associates." She had her hands
in her lap and she began to wring them together. "I had money. So I
thought I would pay off what he owed."

Alys spoke up, shaking her head, "The Leather Aprons? You
presented yourself to the Leather Aprons? As Lydia Ashdown? You
might as well have rung the dinner bell."

Lydia nodded, her delicate chin quivering. "They were horrible,"
she said, her voice barely above a whisper. "They took all that I had
brought, and then told me that it was not enough. I was to bring
more money, every week, or they would kill Calder, and then hurt
my family."

"Why didn't you go home then?" Dax asked. "Why not come to
the magistrates? To me?"

"It would mean leaving Calder behind to face the wrath of
those animals at having lost me." She shook her head vehemently.
"We knew that if we were to get out of Resa, we would need to free
ourselves from the threat of the Leather Aprons once and for all."

"By making them think you were both dead," Dax said.

Lydia nodded. "We were desperate. So, instead of bringing the
latest payment to the Leather Aprons, we came here to the Tigress."

By the closed door, the Tigress gave a slight bow. "And I was of
course more than happy to support such a noble enterprise in any
way I could."

"I've no doubt of that," Alys said. "You supplied the bodies,
then, and arranged safe passage?"

"I am nothing if not resourceful, dear. You of all people should
remember that."

"Calder had it all planned out. He tattooed both of the bodies to resemble ours. His markings and my burn scar." She smiled. "He really is an artist." She paused for a moment to take a deep breath. "Last night, we made sure we were both seen around the docks, then I came here to wait while he placed the two bodies in the river."

Alys crossed her arms over her chest. "Knowing they would surface eventually with enough damage to hide they weren't really you. And the distinguishing markings would be more than enough to convince anyone interested that you were dead."

"That is just what Calder said. So I waited here, but he never came back. Now please, where is Calder?"

Dax looked lost, as if he could not find the right words to break this young girl's heart.

Alys did it for him. "Calder is dead."

Lydia's head rocked back like Alys had hit her with a fist. She shook her head back and forth as tears fell down her face, but then looked to Dax for confirmation. He could only nod, and validate her pain.

Lydia shook, but her sobs had subsided to an eerie calm. Tears fell from her blankly staring eyes. "Then what does it all matter?" she said in a hollow voice. "My Calder is dead."

Inside Alys, a cold voice spoke. *What did she think was going to happen?* it whispered. *A fairy tale ending? Riding off into the sunset like a troubadour's tale? This was the only way it was going to end. How it was always going to end. There are no happy endings in Lowside.*

Alys turned her back and walked from the room and out into the Lowside night.

A few moments later, Dax came out to join her, his eyes red. She sighed. That was always his problem. He felt too much. Cared too much.

"You should be happy," Alys said. "Young Lady Ashdown is alive, and the only casualties were a few gangers and a degenerate Lowside wastrel that no one is going to miss."

"Lydia will miss him," Dax said simply.

"Then she's a dreamer and a fool," Alys replied.

"She was in love."

"So that makes everything all right? Their entire plan was idiocy and ineptitude. It got him killed and it came close to ending her. You don't think that was foolish?"

"I think it was brave"

"Of course you would."

"They were far braver than we were," he said. "Braver than I was."

Alys looked at him, surprised at the admission. She wanted to return with a barbed tongue, but instead honesty came forth from her mouth. "We were plenty brave, Dax. We just weren't smart."

"We're smarter now."

That caught her off guard. "Are we?" she asked, raising an eyebrow.

Dax smiled. A confident smile with a hint of something hiding behind the edge of it. That confidence was something she hadn't seen in a while. Not since the days when they had first met.

"I'm thinking about spending more time down here in Second District," he said, still wearing that smile.

Alys laughed. "In Lowside? Well, that proves you're an even bigger fool than before, not less of one."

"Perhaps," Dax said. "Then that's all the more reason why I will need to call on you as my occasional guide."

"If you are willing to provide payment," she said, her arms once more crossed, "perhaps I'll help you. For a price of course."

Dax laughed and nodded slowly. "Nothing free in Lowside?"

"Not ever," she said. "And, speaking of which, it's time to pay up, isn't it, Inspector? I believe the terms were for the name of the Justicar for Lowside, and what leverage there is on him."

"Very well," Dax replied. "The name of the new Justicar for the Second District is Lord Daxton Ellis. And as for what leverage there is on him, well..." He paused and looked at her. "You already know."

In stunned silence, Alys watched Dax turn and walk away into the last light of the evening, heading back toward Highside. She watched him until he was gone from her view. And then, as she stepped into the shadowed alley, a slow smile began to grow on her face.

Follow the continuing stories of Alys in Book 2.
Coming Soon.

AUTHOR'S NOTE
ECHOES OF THE ASCENDED, BOOKS 1

Thank you so much for reading *Best Left in the Shadows.*

Mark and I met more than twenty-five years ago, and inspired by all the great fantasy authors of our childhood, we wanted, more than anything, to tell our stories as well. To share them with others. With you.

It has been a long journey to finally get here. It hasn't been easy, but nothing worthwhile ever is.

We've got many more stories to tell in Aedaron. Our mission is to get one new story out to you every month.

Different characters. Different stories. But our same love for the world, characters, drama, and action that matter most to us.

We hope you'll come along for the ride.

– Check us out at gelineauandking.com
– Like us at facebook.com/gelineauandking
– Follow us on Twitter @gelineauandking

Or send us your best wishes via astral projection. Whatever your medium, we accept love in all its forms.

Hope to see you again soon.

Mark & Joe

PREVIEWS
FAITH AND MOONLIGHT

Roan

The smell of the fire still clung to the boy.

It clung to all of his friends as well, filling the space of the small wagon they slept in. In spite of the open top, in spite of the cold breeze that blew throughout the day, even in spite of the two weeks that had passed since the night the orphanage burned down, the children still carried the smell with them. The scent of soot and ashes, of fear and death.

The loss of the orphanage weighed on him more than he thought it would. It had not been much, but in the two years he had been there, it had been more of a home than he had ever known. It had been where he first met the others, and where they welcomed him in as family.

And now, they had all lost everything.

Roan slammed his hand against the wagon's side, the coarse-grained wood biting into his knuckles. In the cold, quiet of the late evening, the sound of it was like a crack of thunder, and immediately he regretted it.-

"Can't sleep?" Kay's dark brown eyes shined in the low light.

"Did I wake you?" he whispered.

"No," she said, rubbing her eyes sleepily as she sat up. Her long brown hair had fallen forward, obscuring her face. Her features were soft and pale, accentuated by large, bright eyes that seemed to take in everything at once. He had always thought she was beautiful.

"I did. I'm sorry, Kay," he said, keeping his voice low. "Go back to sleep."

"What's wrong?" she asked, shifting more upright, a slight edge of tension in her voice.

"Nothing. Just excitement, I guess. Cadell says we should arrive at Resa the day after tomorrow." He gestured toward the only adult in the wagon, the old man handling the reins of the mule team that pulled the wagon. The back of his bald head was wrinkled and marred with small scars and dark, tattooed lines.

Kay's eyes narrowed. "Do you really think we can trust him? That he's telling the truth about starting new lives there?" she asked. "I mean, after everything, how can we trust anything?"

"He did save our lives," he reminded her gently.

"And you saved his."

"Well, that means we should be able to trust each other, don't you think?"

Kay was quiet for a moment. "I guess so," she said, but there was no confidence in her words.

In the half-light, she looked smaller. Diminished. The suspicion and doubt in her voice hurt Roan in his heart. Kay had always seen the best in people. She had always been the first to smile. The first to trust.

But that was before the fire.

Roan reached out and Kay moved to sit beside him. She seemed so small as she settled in. He tousled her hair in an effort to try and cheer her. "Come on. There are great things ahead for us. We're going to become Razors. Like the great heroes in Elinor's stories."

The wagon rocked slowly and both looked to Elinor asleep on the floor, Alys and Ferran beside her. Roan felt a twinge of sadness at the thought of separating from his friends after they had been through so much.

Almost as if she could read his thoughts, Kay sighed. "I wish they could come with us," she whispered.

Roan slowly nodded. "Me too, but they won't be too far away. And they'll be following their dreams. Making them come true, just like we are."

"Are we, Roan?" Kay asked. "How? Other than kitchen chores, I've never held a blade in my life. How am I going to become some great warrior?"

"That's what the school is for," he chided her gently. "They'll handle teaching us and Cadell said he will give us a letter of introduction, so they will give us a chance. That chance is all we need."

Even as he spoke, he hated himself for lying. Kay was right. She had no experience fighting, and she would be going up against the best in the kingdom, students who trained their entire lives for that one sole purpose. She had little chance of making it. And if she didn't, if she failed, then she would truly have nothing.

But what choice did they have?

"What if I don't make it?" Kay said quietly.

"You will."

"How do you know that?"

"Because I'll make sure you do," he said. "I'll be there by your side."

There was a pleading look in her eyes. "And if we fail?"

His lips tight, Roan locked eyes with her. "Then we face whatever comes after. Together."

Kay found his hand and gripped it tightly with both hands. Roan squeezed back. She nodded softly, and then laid her head on his shoulder. He could hear her soft breathing and in a few moments, she was asleep again.

Despite her warmth, Roan felt cold.

His mind brought forth memories of childhood, of being on the ragged edge, fighting for every mouthful of food, desperation turning you into a wild, feral thing that was barely human. That had been life, until Kay and the others took him in. He could not allow her to fall into that existence. It would change her. It would break her. As he had seen it happen to so many others.

No. He couldn't let it come to that.

He wouldn't let it come to that.

She had saved him. Now, he would do the same for her.

He wrapped his arms around her and stayed perfectly still as she slept. The thud of the team's hoofbeats seemed to count down the moments remaining in their journey to Resa, the capital, and to the Razor School of Faith, where their new lives awaited.

A Reaper of Stone

PROLOGUE

Conbert's hands were slick with sweat on the reins, despite the cold breeze. Every rustle of the long yellow grass, every whistle of the wind, any sound not the rhythmic clop of his horse's hooves on the worn cobblestone road sent his eyes darting and heart racing.

He had traveled the Reach Road two times previous. Each time had been without incident. Each time, he had arrived at his destination hale and whole, without even a glimpse of the fabled predators the grasslands were so famous for. Yet each time, the sense of dread, of cold fear, had been with him.

The first time, he had tried to play the part of the brave hero, riding forth on a grand quest like the legendary figures in the old stories. That lasted until he caught sight of the infamous drowning grass. The blades were the height of a man and they moved with a sinuous and lifelike grace on each side of the wide stone road.

The fear had started then, shattering whatever myth he might have fabricated of Conbert Eylnen, the future valiant officer of the King's Own. In the face of that grass and what he knew could be hiding under it, he was just Con, apprentice engineer and architect, student of the academy, and anxious to get the hell out of there.

Somewhere far out across the sea of grass, a lone tree rose up like an island. It marked the halfway point in crossing the grassland. It had often given Con comfort. But this time, beneath the shade of its heavy, twisted boughs, there was movement.

A human shape.

Impossible. The only road through the drowning grass was the one he was on now. No one would be stupid enough to travel into the middle of the cursed grass, set up like a picnic for the rendworms.

Con pulled his horse to a halt. Reaching down to the heavy saddlebag, he pulled out his surveyor's glass and raised the delicate instrument to his eye.

Sure enough, there was a person. A girl. She seemed tall, but even with the glass, it was difficult to judge at this distance. She had short, blonde hair that was almost white as it ruffled in the wind. What really caught his attention was her clothing: the familiar grays of an academy cadet. The same grays he had worn as an underclassman a year ago.

The fear came back, but this time wild. The girl was doomed, marooned at that tree surely as any castaway on a lost island. It was only a matter of time until the rendworms caught wind of her.

Before he knew what he was doing, Con urged his horse into a gallop, off the stone road and into the undulating grass. His breath rasped and tears blurred his eyes.

From the wind, he thought. Tears because of the wind. Not because I am stupid and going to die out here.

He rode hard across the grassland, the twisted spire of the tree ahead of him. As it drew closer, he saw the cadet had caught sight of him. She waved frantically. Conbert focused on her desperate movements, shoring up his rapidly disappearing courage with the knowledge that he was her only hope.

Something brushed his leg and he almost shrieked, but realized it was only a heavy stalk of grass. The tree and the waving girl were a few lengths away now.

Con leaped from the saddle, stumbled, and fell on his face, but he got up quickly. Breathlessly, he stood before the girl. "It's alright, cadet," he gasped. "I can take you out—"

Her hand shot out, covering his mouth. It was almost too fast to follow and his eyes widened with shock.

The cadet met his gaze with a cold, hard look of her own. There was a focus there and not the desperate gratitude Con had expected. Slowly, she raised her free hand and laid a single finger against her lips.

Utterly confused, he could only nod.

She cocked her head, listening. Tall and fairly thin, she was not a delicate beauty. Her features were too strong, too sharp for that, but her clear, blue eyes were vibrant as she searched the grass around them. She sighed and released the hand over his mouth.

Con drew a deep breath. "Cadet, what are you doing out here?"

The girl turned and then, appearing to notice the black and silver uniform, snapped to a smart salute. "Forgive me, sir. I was hunting a rendworm."

"You're what? Are you absolutely mad, girl?" he asked, his voice rising.

"No, sir. Not at all. I am merely here to honor the First Trial of Aedan," she said, bowing her head momentarily. "I am not to return without the jaw of a rendworm, but so far, none have appeared."

"The First Trial of Aedan?"

Con's eyes grew wider. The Hunt. The joke upperclassmen played on first-year cadets at the Academy. The older students regaled them with stories of the First King, Aedan, and the legend of how he bested a field of colossal rendworms to earn a meeting with an ancient one, the Shepherd of Tree and Stone.

Only there was no Hunt.

It was all an elaborate ruse, a traditional jape each first-year cadet class went through. The cadets were stopped at the gate of the Academy, chased and beaten by older cadets wielding sticks and wearing garish costumes. And then the ale casks were brought out and everyone would get ripping drunk.

No one ever actually went out to hunt the damn things.

He looked at the girl again. For her to be out here meant she must have been very sheltered or very stupid. But that didn't explain why the other cadets wouldn't have stopped her at the gate.

Conbert felt suddenly cold. Had they done this on purpose? Had they sent her unknowingly to her death? The chill turned to anger. The Academy had never been a warm place, but it had never been this cruel.

Conbert opened his mouth to tell the girl the truth about her fool's errand, but saw her posture change. She stood absolutely still, looking past him, a long-handled black mace in one hand. His horse danced skittishly as the grass waved around it.

The girl put a hand on his shoulder. Her voice was low. "Whatever happens next, you mustn't move."

And then the ground underneath the horse exploded and a pale white form the size of a wagon erupted into the air. The horse let out a scream that turned into a wet gurgle as white writhing tentacles enveloped the animal. The copper tang of blood filled the air and Conbert felt his stomach lurch.

He thought to go for the sword at his side, but he saw the girl's eyes.

He held himself still as another of the creatures breached the drowning grass. It was a huge mass of rippling white flesh, except at the front, where the mouth opened like an exposed wound. Massive tearing fangs lined the pink maw, and white tentacles writhed from the worm's throat, seeking the remnants of the thrashing horse. The two monsters tore the horse apart in seconds, powerful tentacles flaying meat from bone with horrific efficiency.

As the rendworms began to slide across the ground in their direction, Con felt a terror urging him to run. He fought against it, trying to focus instead on the perfect stillness of the young girl as the huge worms slid past them.

Then the girl moved.

The young cadet was fast and sure as she darted forward. She struck out with the mace, swinging it with both hands, and smashing it into the rendworm's side. There was a loud crack, and Con knew that somewhere inside the sinuous horror, a bone had broken under the blow.

The rendworm let out a keening screech that stabbed Con's ears and took the breath from his lungs. The injured creature folded its bulk around, trying to round on the girl. The crown of white tentacles snapped and writhed like angry serpents, seeking her.

Instead of retreating, she moved into the circle of the rendworm's turning bulk. The mace carved through the air once more, the flanged head crashing squarely just behind the enormous hooked jaws and tentacles. This time, there was no crack like thunder, but a wet sound like the smashing of rotting fruit. The rendworm immediately shuddered and collapsed to the ground dead.

The other rendworm came now, covering Con with a shower of earth, a massive shadow blocking out the sun. Bringing his blade free of its sheath, he held it before him in desperation as one of the tentacles lashed at him. By some fortune, Con's sword came across his body right in the path of the slashing tooth of the tentacle. Con dropped to the ground as the horror reared for another strike.

There was an explosion of gore as the creature's soft abdomen was crushed under the girl's mace. The white flesh shuddered and collapsed, and Con scrambled away from the new corpse. Through the noxious rendworm blood dripping down his face, he peered at the young cadet.

Her eyes shone with excitement and triumph.

"From the stories, I thought they would be bigger," the girl said, her voice colored in disappointment.

Conbert looked at her, unable to stop shaking, unable to keep from staring as she handed him a water flask. She walked to the first corpse and began working away at the creature with the short blade from her belt. With quick, sure movements, she tore free the huge serrated jaws of the rendworm.

The girl grinned ear to ear. "They have no eyes, but they can feel your vibrations when you move. You did incredibly well, sir."

Con could only nod dumbly. Finally, he found his tongue. "Conbert Eylnen," he said, unsure of what else to say. "My name is Con."

The cadet nodded as she tore out the jaw of the second rendworm. "Elinor," she said, handing him the bloody mandible. "That one's yours, but I think we had better get on our way before we attract any more attention. Don't you agree?"

Con shook his head in disbelief. "After you," he finally managed.

Elinor smiled and started for the road.

Con made sure to follow close behind.

Rend the Dark

PROLOGUE

THE BOY FELT IT BEFORE he saw it.

There was a chill feeling, different from the usual cold that filled the stone halls of the orphanage. That cold was familiar and simple. You felt it in your bones. You endured it by hovering closer to the kitchen fire before the matron caught you, or by sharing a blanket with your chosen brothers and sisters.

But this was different. This was a sharp-edged cold. Like the glitter that came off the knife they used to kill the goats. Like the ice that sheathed the old tree outside and made the branches snap off. He did not feel this cold in his bones, but in his very soul. And it made him want to whimper with fear.

He had tried to keep quiet. Already many of the other orphans were angry at him. The dancers and jugglers had them clapping and laughing, a rare treat for the forgotten children housed here.

Until he had begun screaming and pointing at one of the performers.

He had ruined the show, and the embarrassed matron sent the children off to their dormitories immediately. Their anger was palpable, a terrible thing he felt all around, and he could hear harsh whispers up and down the halls of the old fortress that served as the orphanage. "Crazy is at it again," he heard. "The lunatic's seeing monsters again." He knew if not for his friends, he would have suffered that night.

His friends Elinor, Alys, Roan, and Kay had not been angry, though. They believed him. They comforted him, drawing him away from the performers and out of the room without a look back at the ruined entertainment. Elinor wrapped an arm around his shoulders as they walked and Roan stared daggers at the other orphans, defying their anger at his friend. Together, they returned to the dormitory and prepared for bed.

No, his friends had not been angry like the other children were. They never were. But he also knew they did not understand. Not truly. Even he began to doubt himself. Perhaps the cruel whispers from the other children were right, he thought.

Until tonight. Until he had seen the blackheart just an arm's length away from him and he screamed and screamed till his throat was raw. Where their hearts should have been, oily mud and black smoke oozed from their chests to cover their bodies. He had seen them three times before, but never up close like this.

Even now, in the small hours of the night when everyone in the large room was asleep, the boy remained awake. The fear of the shadowed juggler would not leave him, and behind his closed eyes, he pictured the horrible darkness moving over the man. The feeling crept over him more and more. The cold feeling. Sharp. Dangerous.

He finally could not stand it any longer. His eyes snapped open, and he looked across the darkened room, past the simple cots the orphans all slept on.

And he saw it.

The blackheart was in the room. The rolling, oily blackness spilled from its chest like blood from a wound, deeper even than the dark of the night. It stood across the room from him, looming over the foot of one girl's bed. The boy felt his heart pounding, and he longed to reach out

2

to touch his friends, either to wake them to see what he saw or to wake himself from what must be a nightmare. But he was too frightened to move.

As he watched, the juggler's shape sloughed off, dropping to the floor like a discarded garment. In its place was something more horrifying. The head became longer and had no eyes, only a round mouth from which the boy could see wicked teeth. It craned a long, serpent-like neck toward the sleeping child while reaching forward with ragged claws at the end of spindly arms. The thing bent down to feed, and the boy moaned with terror.

The long neck whipped impossibly around, turning its eyeless face toward the boy. It dropped to all fours and charged across the room.

For the second time that night the boy screamed himself raw.

***

Ferran opened his eyes and tried to still his breathing. The room was warm. All around him were men and women, wearing the earthy colors favored by the Order of Talan. Many of them had their exposed skin heavily tattooed with strange symbols and designs. But all of them looked on him with understanding eyes.

An old man stepped forward, leaning heavily on a cane. Dark stripes were inked onto his weathered and wrinkled face, contrasting with the bright white of his long beard. He stood before Ferran and watched as the young man drew deep breaths.

"What did you see?" the old man asked.

Ferran matched the old man's gaze and steadied himself. "My past," Ferran said.

The old man studied him for a long moment and then nodded once. He stepped out of the way and made a gesture. Across the length of the chamber, a heavy iron door swung open, to reveal the creature from his memory. The monstrous head whipped around and the circular maw puckered at the air. Long talons scraped across the floor with a high-pitched keening as it drew away from the open door.

"What do you see?" the old man asked from behind Ferran.

In his left hand, Ferran felt the weight of a long length of silver chain, and he let one end fall to the floor with a clear, bright ring. His other hand tightened around the haft of a short spear, the blade held before him, catching the light of the torches carried by the members of the Order who looked on.

"What do you see?" the old man asked once more.

Ferran's lips drew back into a savage smile. "My future," he said and advanced on the monster.

A Reaper of Stone

A Lady is dead. Her noble line ended. And the King's Reaper has come to reclaim her land and her home. In the marches of Aedaron, only one thing is for certain. All keeps of the old world must fall.

Elinor struggles to find her place in the new world. She once dreamed of great things. Of becoming a hero in the ways of the old world. But now she is a Reaper. And her duty is clear. Destroy the old. Herald the new.

"A classic fantasy tale with a strong, admirable heroine and a nice emotional punch. Great start to an enjoyable new series!"
– RL King, author of *The Alastair Stone Chronicles*

"A Reaper of Stone has the essence of a traditional fantasy epic, full of adventure and beautiful, lyrical prose, in well under a hundred pages."
– *Books by Proxy*

Rend the Dark

The great Ruins are gone. The titans. The behemoths. All banished to the Dark and nearly forgotten. But the cunning ones, the patient ones remain. They hide not in the cracks of the earth or in the shadows of the world. But inside us. Wearing our skin. Waiting. Watching.

Once haunted by visions of the world beyond, Ferran now wields that power to hunt the very monsters that he once feared. He is not alone. Others bear the same terrible burden. But Hunter or hunted, it makes no difference. Eventually, everything returns to the Dark.

"Atmospheric, fast paced, engaging quick read, with a satisfying story and glimpses of Supernatural *and King's* IT.*"

– BooksChatter

BEST LEFT IN THE SHADOWS

A Highside girl. Beaten. Murdered. Her body found on a Lowside dock. A magistrate comes looking for answers. For justice.

Alys trades and sells secrets among the gangs and factions of Lowside. She is a daughter of the underworld. Bold. Cunning. Free. When an old lover asks for help, she agrees. For a price.

Together, they travel into the dark heart of the underworld in search of a killer.

"I was blown away by the detail and world building that was accomplished in so few pages. I didn't feel like I was seeing a section of a puzzle, more like I was reading a story that would contribute to a larger whole, but is compelling and rich all on its own."

— *Mama Reads, Hazel Sleeps*

Faith and Moonlight

Roan and Kay are orphans.

A fire destroys their old life, but they have one chance to enter the School of Faith.

They are given one month to pass the entry trials, but as Roan excels and Kay fails, their devotion to each other is put to the test.

They swore they would face everything together, but when the stakes are losing the life they've always dreamed of, what will they do to stay together?

What won't they do?

"You can really feel Roan's desire and dream to be something more and you can also feel Kay's frustration and struggle. And underneath all that you can practically touch how much they care about each other."

– White Sky Project

Made in the USA
San Bernardino, CA
27 April 2019